The Little Christmas Angel

by Peggy Barons

Illustrated by Izzy Bean

Carpenter's Son Publishing

Many thanks to my sister, Kay, for giving me the idea to write my own story. Much love and gratitude to my husband, Mark, for his support and encouragement and to our four children, for reminding me how much fun they had searching for our own Christmas Angel. I hope my two grandsons, Oliver and Archie (and any future grands), will enjoy this tradition as much as we have. I also owe a world of thanks to my own mom and dad for always giving our family a happy Christmas!

The Little Christmas Angel

©2016 by Peggy Barons

Published by Carpenter's Son Publishing, Franklin, Tennessee, in association with Larry Carpenter of Christian Book Services, LLC. www.christianbookservices.com

Illustrations by Izzy Bean

Edited by Gail Fallen

Cover and Interior Layout Design by Suzanne Lawing

Printed in China

978-1-942587-50-7

In the little town of Bethlehem, long, long ago,
a very special baby was born, whom we've all come to know.

He was born in a stable with animals all around.

Angels came to greet him, and sang *heavenly* sounds.

One little angel was too young to fly far,
so she stayed in the fields, watching the bright star.

"What shall I do on this **Oh Holy Night**?"
she said to herself, fixing her halo just right.

"I can't get to the manger, but there must be a plan;
I'll flutter up high, as high as I can!"

But all she could see, from her perch not so high,
were some sad shepherds and lambs, and she thought, "Oh my!"
She said, "This is not right," as she started to fall,
"This night is great, the greatest of all!"

So she gathered up all of the strength she could gather and zipped over their heads, sprinkling heavenly matter.

All at once they were filled with Christmassy joy,
and suddenly, she knew what to do, for each girl and boy.

All through Bethlehem and the cities back then . . .

And to your town, too, she flies, again and again.

She flies through kitchens and bedrooms

and playrooms with toys.
She sprinkles and sparkles, scattering great joys.

Up the stairs and down the hall,
to all living creatures . . .

Both great

. . . and small.

She lands in one spot, just before dawn.
And you never know what, she just might land on.

Oh, you'll know what room, you can feel it inside.

That room is cheery and happy and bright!

And on Christmas Eve,
the holiest of nights,

the angel takes off on one final flight.